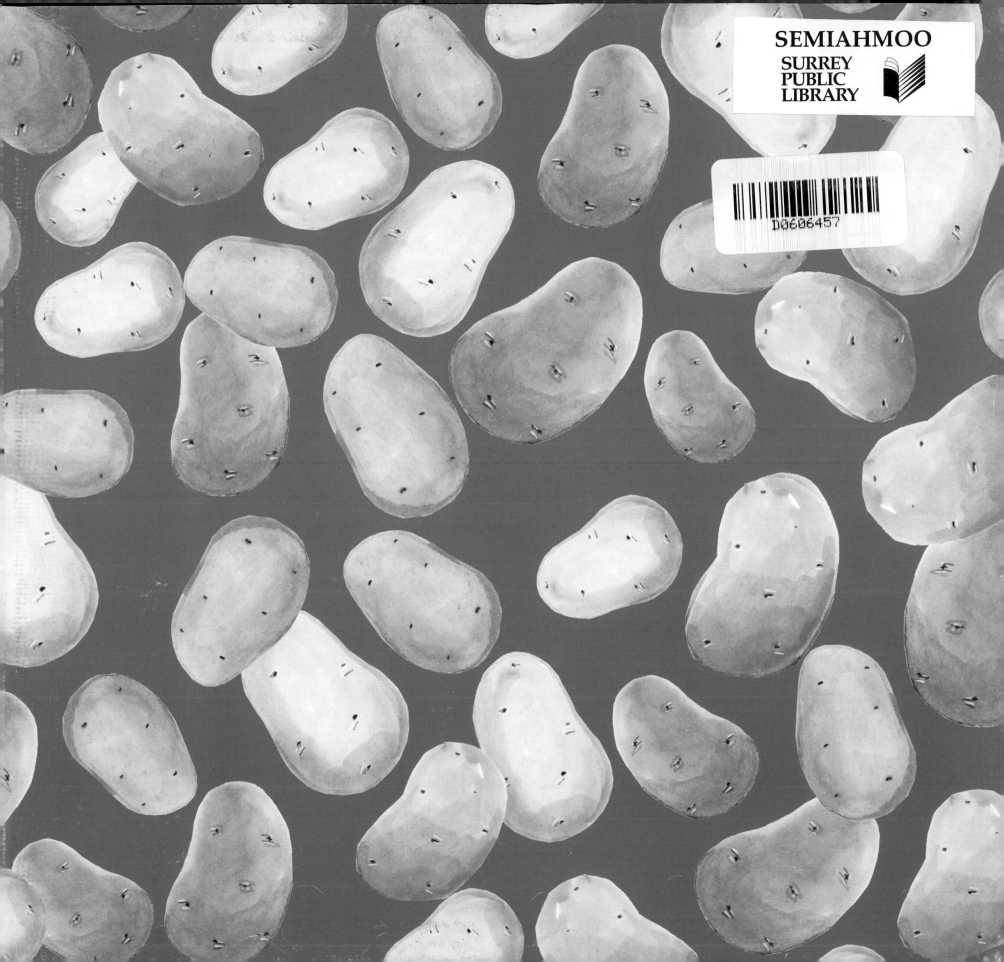

The Greatest Potatoes

by Penelope Stowell

pictures by Sharon Watts

JUMP AT THE SUN

HYPERION BOOKS FOR CHILDREN

NEW YORK

For my son, Andres—P.S.

To my grandfathers, Vernon and Paul,
who shared both their knowledge
and their chips with me—S.W.

Printed in Hong Kong   Reinforced binding   First Edition   1 3 5 7 9 10 8 6 4 2

This book is set in Bernhard Gothic.

Library of Congress Cataloging-in-Publication Data on file.

ISBN 0-7868-5113-9

Visit www.hyperionbooksforchildren.com

The finicky and fussy Commodore Cornelius Vanderbilt loved potatoes.
So he went on a mission to find the greatest potato dish ever!

Vanderbilt traveled from continent to continent, but he hated how the potatoes were prepared everywhere he went. Customers noticed the bad reviews and fled the restaurants, and Vanderbilt left a salty stream of tears in his wake.

Today Vanderbilt was back in America—and he was headed straight for Cary Moon's Lake House Restaurant in Saratoga, where the headlines said it all.

It was more than Head Chef Pierre Contraire could bear. He passed out on the spot.

The vegetable chef, Stewie Chewy, went home sick.

And that left only the fry cook, George Crum.

"You're my last hope, George," said Mr. Moon, the owner and *maître d'hôtel*. "How are you at cooking potatoes?"

"Don't worry," George said proudly, "I make the best french-fried potatoes in the world."

"French fries? . . . We're doomed!" Mr. Moon cried. He locked himself in his office to work on his résumé.

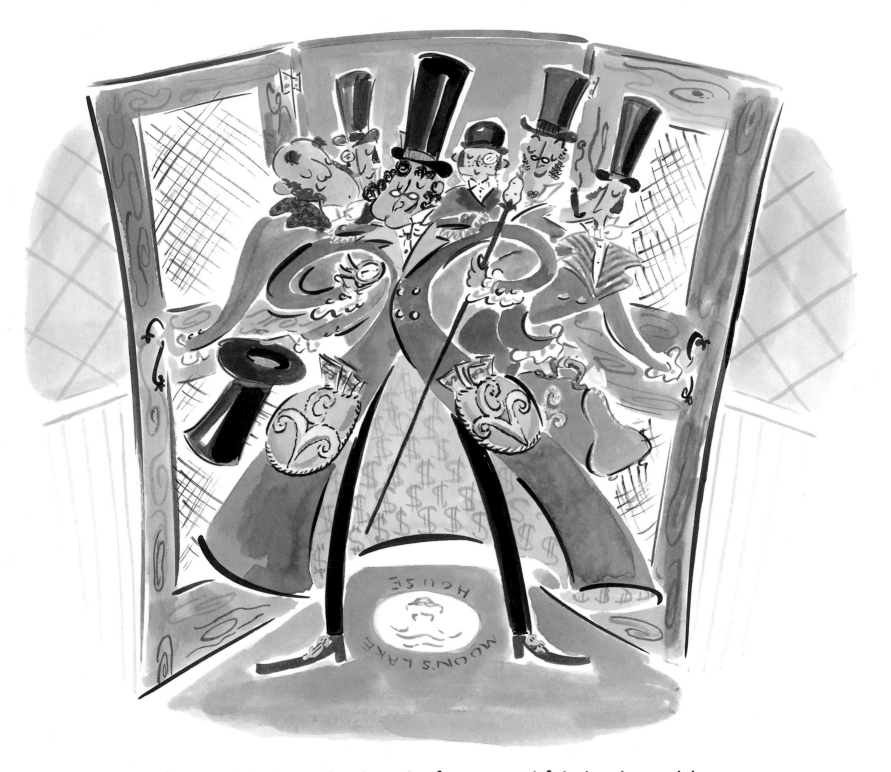

At six o'clock on the dot, the famous and fabulously wealthy
Cornelius Vanderbilt swept into the lodge with his attendants in tow.

Vanderbilt adjusted his pince-nez and coughed.
"I'll have potatoes," he announced.
"Yes, sir," said Cary Moon. *"CRUM!"*

"CRUM!"

Back in the kitchen, George got to work.

CHOP!

SIZZLE!

FIZZLE!

The potatoes cooked to a perfect golden brown.

George brought out a plate of his finest french fries and laid it before the commodore. *"Bon appétit,"* he said.

But Vanderbilt turned up his nose.

"These are worse than the baked potatoes at Murphy's, which we promptly roasted!" His entire entourage sniggered, their noses high in the air.

George scratched his head. Had he made a *faux pas*?

"Let me try again, Commodore," George insisted.

SMASH! HASH! CRASH!

George returned with a plate of lightly browned and peppered potatoes.

The ornery old Vanderbilt shoved the plate away. "Yuck! Utterly inedible! Even the Congress Hall hash browns had more constitution." His cronies snuffled and snorted (and sneezed) in agreement.

Some customers noticed the commotion and left.

George thought everybody loved french-fried potatoes. Or did Cornelius Vanderbilt simply delight in disliking things? George aimed to find out *tout de suite*.

Peel! Slice! Dice!

"No! No!" Vanderbilt huffed.
"Too thick! That fare is foul!"

SCRAPE! Bake! SMOOSH!
Vanderbilt waved them off.
"What vile vegetables!
No flavor at all!"

Cary Moon packed his bags. George Crum grumbled, "If that Cornelius Vanderbilt can't tell a good french fry when he tastes one . . .

". . . If that persnickety old commodore wants a BAD potato . . .
well, then, that's EXACTLY what he's going to get!"

Zip!

George was down to his very last spud. He sharpened his best kitchen cleaver
and peeled the potato. *Zip!* He cut it so finely that the paper-thin slices seemed
to disappear. "'Too thick'?" he laughed. "Ha!"

Then he dropped the potatoes *plop!* into hissing cooking oil.
The potatoes shriveled up and turned dry and brown. **FWWP!**
"'Utterly inedible'?" snickered George. "Hee!"

Last, he put a dash of salt on them. Then a splash more. SHAKE-SHAKE-SHAKE!
He put so much salt on the chips that they sparkled. "'No flavor'?" giggled
George. "Hoo!"

George Crum strode to Cornelius Vanderbilt's table. He plopped the plate in front of the old curmudgeon.

Maybe these *will remove the bitterness from Cornelius Vanderbilt's mouth,* he thought.

Vanderbilt poked one with his fork, but it shattered into a million pieces. POOF!
He lifted another crisp high above his face, inspected it, and bit down. CRACK!
"Hmm," he said. Then he tried to eat the rest of it. CRUMBLE!

He picked up another chip. **CHOMP!** Crumbs flew everywhere.
Then he attacked another one. **Munch!** Another. **CRUNCH!**
Cornelius Vanderbilt couldn't eat just one!

"What are these called, Crum?" he sputtered over the din of crisp, crunchy potatoes crackling in his ears!

He ate the whole plateful! Then he demanded . . . more? Yes!

He pounded the table. "MORE! On the double!"

He just couldn't stop!

Mr. Moon ran to the store and bought up every last potato he could find. He brought them to his right-hand man, the new head cook, Master Chef George Crum.

George spent that night, and all the weeks that followed, preparing flaky fried potato crisps for Cornelius Vanderbilt . . .

. . . until he opened up his own restaurant. Soon word spread across the globe about how he'd quenched Cornelius Vanderbilt's hunger for the world's greatest potatoes . . .

. . . and about how he, George Crum, had invented the greatest snack food ever known.

Author's Note

GEORGE CRUM'S FATHER, ABE SPECK, was an African American jockey from Kentucky. A former slave, Speck headed to upstate New York upon gaining his freedom and married a Native American woman of the Huron Nation from the Adirondack Mountains. Their son, George Crum, preferred mountaineering to cooking, but found work as a chef at the Moon's Lake House Restaurant in the popular resort town of Saratoga, New York, during the summer of 1853.

It is said that George Crum had a short temper and a sharp sense of humor. Legend has it that an irascible customer sorely irritated George Crum by sending his fried potatoes (later to be known simply as "french fries") back to the kitchen time and time again. As a practical joke on him, George created the worst fried potato in the world—too thin, too salty, and so crisp it could not be eaten with a fork. But the customer was enchanted with George's "Saratoga flaky fried potatoes," and the snack caught on.

While the identity of the persnickety patron who ignited George's ire remains up for debate, many claim that the honor belongs to none other than the colorful and salty millionaire Commodore Cornelius Vanderbilt, steamship magnate and railroad entrepreneur, and a frequent visitor to the Moon's Lake House Restaurant during that time.

The Saratoga flaky fried potato became so popular, George eventually opened up his own restaurant in Saratoga, serving up his famous creation to delighted customers. Today, more than 150 years after its invention, George's practical joke has evolved into the most popular snack food in America—everybody's favorite, the POTATO CHIP.

Great Potato Chip Recipe

serves 4—6

4 russet potatoes
cooking oil
salt

child: Wash and peel the potatoes.

adult: Using a mandoline vegetable slicer, the long edge of a grater, or a sharp kitchen knife, slice the potatoes evenly and as paper-thin as possible.

child: Soak the potato slices in cold water for 10—15 minutes, then rinse until water runs clear. (This step keeps the potatoes from becoming too brown during the frying process.)

child: Dry potato slices by spinning them in a salad spinner. (George Crum didn't have a salad spinner and dried his potato slices by spreading them out on a rack in a low oven set to 200° F, leaving the door open to dry off the chips. Ask an adult for help.)

adult: Fill a deep fat fryer one-third of the way with cooking oil, and heat the oil to 330—350° F. Drop a handful of chips into the fry basket and fry in cooking oil for 3—4 minutes or until they turn golden brown. Remove basket and empty chips onto paper towels to drain and cool.

child: Salt very lightly.

Repeat all steps until every potato slice is cooked.

TIPS FOR ALTERNATE COOKING METHODS:

Some people prefer baked potato chips to fried potato chips. Place the potato slices in a single layer on a well-greased cookie sheet and bake at 350° F for about 10 minutes, turning often. As the chips brown, remove from the cookie sheet one by one until the batch is done. Repeat and enjoy!

SELECTED BIBLIOGRAPHY

Gibbs, C.R. *The Afro-American Inventor.* Washington, D.C.: Gibbs, 1975.

Harmon, John E. *Atlas of Popular Culture in the Northeastern United States.* New Britain, Conn.: Central Connecticut State University, 1998. Available online at www.geography.ccsu.edu/harmonj/atlas/potchips.htm.

Hotaling, Edward. *They're Off! Horse Racing in Saratoga.* Syracuse, N.Y.: Syracuse University Press, 1995.

Lane, Wheaton J. *Commodore Vanderbilt: An Epic of the Steam Age.* New York: Knopf, 1942.

Mitchell, David. Text of presentation for Object ID 1991.118.0001. Brookside Museum (Saratoga County Historical Society), Ballston Spa, N.Y., 1992.

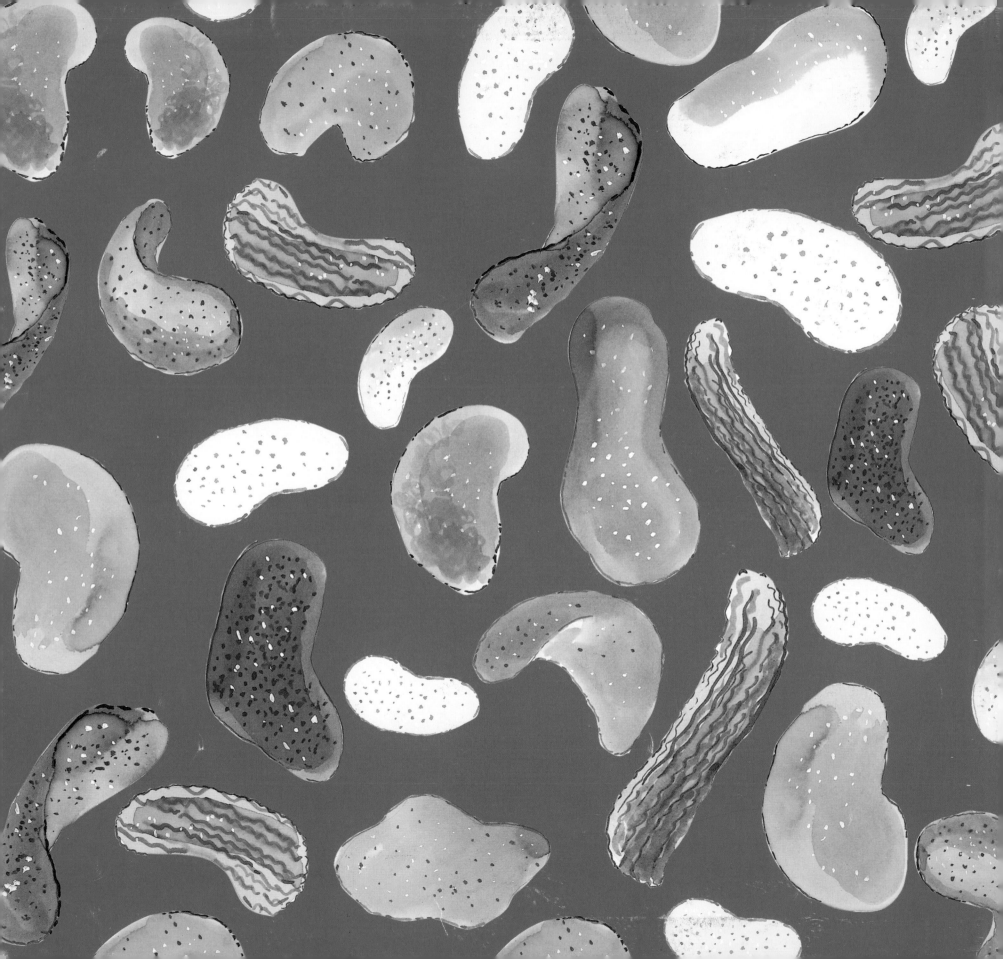